Reclaiming Near and Dear Stories

Samuel Fleming

ISBN-13: 978-1-7359407-6-2 (paperback)
ISBN-13: 978-1-7359407-5-5 (ebook)

Thank you to my Beta Readers

And, as always, to my First Reader,

Mel.

Contents

Aunt Millie's House

Introduction

I lost someone—someone magical—and I don't know how to feel about it.

When I was a girl, I spent weeks at my Aunt Millie's house. She lived out in the country, up in the mountains. When mom drove me, I knew we were close because minutes would pass in between houses and if you weren't paying attention you might miss them altogether. The final twenty minutes was nothing but trees and an endless dirt road. Then Aunt Millie's house would appear around the corner, like some lost magical place we'd stumbled on in the forest.

Mom and Aunt Millie would mill about and talk in the kitchen just like they talked on the phone; laughing about "the old days" back when both of them lived out here in the woods instead of just Aunt Millie. I think they had an aversion to chairs: My mom because of the long drive and my aunt because she was a writer and sat "all the damn time."

All the while I would stand at the back door and stare through the glass at the forest beyond, only vaguely aware of their conversation (and subconsciously sharing their aversion to sitting). Even though the house was in the mountains, it was flat for a while around Millie's house. The trees were tall and the woods so dense it was like a great big curtain that walled off her house from the world. You couldn't even see the sky.

I was a patient kid. Eventually mom would make me come over and tell Aunt Millie about school. I guess she thought that I didn't talk to Aunt Millie enough, but that wasn't it. Aunt Millie and I both knew that we had all week to talk and that there was "time enough for that" after I played in the woods. So eventually Millie would tell me to hug my mom and go outside and play until dinner.

* * *

The Woods

I loved those woods. From that first week until the last.

Growing up with those weeks at Aunt Millie's was like being in love and I don't think I ever felt so strongly about a place or the people around it as I did at Millie's house. There were weeks where I was so overcome with beauty and awe that I couldn't speak and other weeks (in my teenage years) when I was self-absorbed and couldn't be bothered—but we'll get to that later.

When I was little those woods were another world and the backdoor of the house was my portal. I stepped into those woods and it was like I walked into a fantasy world. The trees, tall and rough, most with branches far too high up to climb. The grass was thick and green. All around birds called out and crickets chirped somewhere in the grass.

It reminded me of the city—I know, a strange comparison, but it did. The forest was its own little city. The trees were skyscrapers, the grass was roads between them. The birds and crickets were people. I admit, the metaphor made more sense when I was a kid.

Anyway, I don't know how deep I used to wander into those woods. I think it was a miracle that I didn't get lost; there weren't any landmarks from my aunt's house to the little stream or to old-man boulder.

Sometimes I think it was because of the fox's fey magic or the good will of the forest that I didn't get lost, or run into a bear.

I was ten. The first day of that first week I was at Millie's was when I met the fox or at least that's what I thought it was; just a little taller than a cat, with slender legs, tall ears and a bushy tail. It had a long face like a fox.

That was where the similarities ended.

When I first saw it I thought the poor thing was tangled up in vines. I ran over to help, but then it darted away, trailing vines and leaves behind it. It was so fast I could barely see its legs. It ran to and fro and then up the side of the tree, and even in spirals around the trunk.

It stopped and clung upside down to the side of the tree and stared at me; its bushy tail wagging in the air. Now it was still enough to get a good look at it:

The fox wasn't really a fox at all. Instead of red fur, the creature's skin was the color and texture of bark. Its hair was sparse, thick and green, like vines. Tiny leaves dropped from the vines. Its face was hairless too and covered with rough bark—like someone had tried carving a fox out of wood.

It was strange, but I guess it didn't seem so strange to a city girl who had never seen a fox before.

Its eyes were wide and bright, and the shifting colors of autumn leaves.

It was panting and smiling at me, reflecting my excitement. Young-me thought it wanted to play. Luckily enough I was right.

It ran around the tree, flowing over the bark like a water droplet. Then it vanished and appeared on another tree a moment later. I tried to keep up.

The fox cackled; a quick, deep laugh like the rumble of a storm cloud cut short. It echoed through the forest. It laughed as we ran. Sometimes the rumbles seemed like they came from all around me and not from the fox.

We played for hours. Chasing each other around the forest. I tried to reach out and touch it a few times when it got close, but it was impossibly quick for young me.

I almost forgot about dinner. It followed me all the way home, but never left the tree line. I waved goodbye, thinking that the fox knew what that meant.

At dinner, I told Aunt Millie all about the fox. At first she was worried, until I told her about how strange it was.

"Oh," Millie said. Her eyes were wide with excitement. "You met a fae." She must have seen the confusion on my face because she continued, "You know: A faerie… What about 'green folk'? No… Well, they're spirits of the forest and you were very lucky to meet one."

"Did you ever meet a green person?"

Millie smiled and took a bite of her dinner roll. "I've lived in these woods for a long, long time. I've met quite a few."

Aunt Millie told me I had to finish my dinner and help her with dishes if I wanted any more answers. I was so excited that I didn't mind.

She told me all about the green folk she met: About the Craobh, living trees that would carve intricate patterns on their own bark. About the moon goddess, Ban Boirie, who painted in the night sky. And about the father of the deer, Arietes, who was so tall that his legs were mistaken for the trees.

I wanted to know more—to know everything about the green folk, but Millie didn't tell me all at once.

After dinner she told me to make up my own stories about the green folk. Just like she did.

We sat on the thick, squishy couch in the living room. We both had a laptop (she let me use her old one). She told me to write a story about the fae fox that I met and to give him a name.

"Doesn't the fox have his own name?" I asked.

"Probably, but I don't think he'll mind being called something else."

I wanted to ask more questions, but Millie told me to write. So I tried.

Back then the words came easily.

That first week I wrote about the fae fox, Shoan, and how we ran through a town of giants. We chased each other all over town, weaving between all the hairy giants' feet. I almost caught him and he almost caught me. Then both our families called us in for dinner.

Aunt Millie read it and told me to add details, like how hairy the giants' feet were, what Shoan looked like, and how excited I was when I nearly caught Shoan.

It was my Aunt Millie who taught me about writing fiction and it was the woods that gave me inspiration.

Each day I would go out in the woods to play with the fae fox. He didn't seem to mind his new name. He just seemed happy to have someone to play with.

Each evening I would come back to the house for dinner and to write with Millie.

I asked her what she wrote about. She said that she used to write about the fae, just like I was doing, but now she wrote about even bigger things.

She had a shelf on the wall of the living room lined with books that all had her name on them; all books that she had written. On the covers were castles and dragons and forests and armies. She said she still wrote about the fae sometimes, but they were a small part of the bigger stories.

I wouldn't understand until I was older that my Aunt Millie was Emily Fiontann, the author of the series *Maon's Valor* and the *Pirates of Lochlann*. If you asked a hundred people on the street if they knew her books, at least a dozen would reply with an enthusiastic yes.

It was fitting that the time I spent in my own head, and writing on the couch next to Millie, was almost as magical as the time spent chasing Shoan.

I can still remember leaving after that first magical week.

I spent the days outside chasing Shoan. I wanted so badly to pick him up and cuddle him like my cat, Grady, back home, but Shoan would have none of it. He was just too fast. I got frustrated and sat on the green grass, sobbing and holding out my arms to him, but he just watched from high up on the tree. When my sobs grew loud, so did his rumbling laugh.

Then Millie called for me and told me to come back inside. My mother would be there soon to take me home.

Shoan followed me all the way back home before disappearing back into the woods.

"Why are you so sad?" Aunt Millie asked.

I told her all about wanting to hug Shoan and how I didn't want to leave. There was something magical about Millie's house. I told her that I would miss it and miss her, and miss Shoan.

My aunt held me close and told me that she and Shoan and the forest would be here waiting for me. She let me take the old laptop back with me so I could keep writing my story about Shoan.

I don't think I had ever felt such a mix of happiness and sadness ever again.

Months passed. I couldn't play in the city like I could in the forest. We lived on a busy one-way street that was even busier with people. I had to be with my friends and with either my mom or another parent. We would play on the patio in front of our townhouse and we could never, ever go past the corners of the block. Usually parents would take us to the playground a few blocks from my house.

I couldn't visit Aunt Millie during the winter because of school and that it was hard to travel when it snowed.

I would run around the playground with my friends and imagine that it was the forest. The legs of the swing set and slide were the great big trees and my friends were Shoan, even though they were much easier to catch.

All the while I didn't stop thinking about fey fox or the forest, and I didn't stop writing. I think I wrote every time I got a spare minute. Before long I had pages and pages of Shoan and I going on adventures: Sometimes we were in Giant Town, other times we were in Millie's forest. I even had a story about smuggling Shoan into school inside my backpack.

My mom would just smile when she saw me plop down in front of the laptop.

"Just like your Aunt Millie."

* * *

Going Back

Each Summer I got to go back to my Aunt Millie's and spend a week at a time up there in that magical forest.

Each time Shoan was waiting for me. It was like I never left. He would cackle like rolling thunder and we would spend the day chasing each other through the giant trees.

It was over those few years that we found the stream and old-man rock. The stream was a little thing, though the water moved quite quickly. Shoan and I would play over the river or scurry around the top of old-man rock.

Old-man rock was a huge, smooth boulder that looked like a bald man's head with a large nose. His eyebrows were wrinkled like he was always deep in thought.

I used to sit and throw pebbles into it and imagine where the river took them. They might end up in a town down the river or tumble into the bottom of the ocean. Or I would sit next to old-man rock. He didn't babble like the river did, so I would sit next to him and try to guess what he was thinking so hard about. Was it the trees? Was it the river? Did he lose his keys?

When I would throw pebbles into the river, sometimes Shoan would lay down and watch. When I took a nap beside old-man rock, Shoan would take a nap beside him too—but never quite close enough to touch.

So it went like that for years' worth of visits to my Aunt Millie's house in the mountains. I would spend my days running through the woods and exploring with Shoan, my green fey fox. Then I would spend the evenings with Millie. Sometimes we would talk, but mostly we would write.

For a few years—my stories grew as I did. My story about smuggling Shoan to school in my backpack continued by taking Shoan all over town and stuffing scraps of my lunch into the backpack to feed him inconspicuously. We would visit Giant Town and take the tiniest boats down the stream, and spend all day asking old-man rock questions which he would spend an equally long amount of time to answer.

In middle school things were different. School was hard and so I had less time to write because there was so much work to do. But school was also hard by virtue of simply being a young girl—no matter what clothes I wore or how quiet I tried to be, sometimes the other girls and boys would make fun of me.

Looking back on those days, I know I had an easier time during school than most did. Being quiet saved me a great deal of trouble. Sometimes I watched groups of girls argue back and forth and call each other horrible names and they seemed like they were yelling at a thunder cloud; no matter how much good yelling seemed like it was doing, the thunder cloud was going to yell back even louder and then rain on you for good measure.

So I needed the escape of writing more and more but had less and less time to escape.

Those days I wanted very badly to run away to Aunt Millie's (even though it was far and I wasn't even sure what direction it was in, much less what road to take). I dreamed of living there, like she did, far away from other people.

I suppose it made it all the better when I got to go to Millie's house in the mountains, but even my Aunt's house wasn't safe from complications.

Sometime in middle school I got my first phone. Without a doubt, having that technology in my pocket was nearly as big a moment of my childhood...well, as finding Shoan in the woods that very first day.

It wasn't so much that smartphones were evil or that social media was evil, it was just that having a phone allowed so much more into my life. Having a phone at my aunt's brought a whole dozen other worlds with me; worlds that competed for my attention.

I still went outside and played with Shoan, especially during middle school—gods, I missed him so much then. Beg as I might, Shoan still wouldn't let me hold him. He always thought my grasping for him was a game of chase rather than a desperate need for touch and affection.

So I chased him and, for a time, we both pretended that nothing had changed. We pretended that I wasn't already inches taller or that I wasn't becoming a young woman instead of the girl that Shoan first met in the woods. We ran to the stream and to old-man rock and took naps.

In the evenings, Millie and I still wrote. I never did keep up with which books she was working on. All I knew was that her shelf of published books kept growing at a steady pace of a book a year.

It was all those spaces in between that those other worlds crept in. It was late nights and rainy days when I couldn't go outside that I would spend on my phone playing games and talking to the few friends I had.

I read stories and books on my phone too—it wasn't all "mindless phony stuff".

That phone was my gateway to reading, and, in a way, reading other people's stories was more damning to my writing than social media or boys or school ever were. I got lost in other people's worlds as much as I did in my own.

Reading was also the way I finally came out of my shell.

The first story I ever read was on a forum—I'm not even sure how I stumbled on it or what the story was called—but it was an old timey pirate story about a pirate captain who attacked a research vessel. They confiscated animals and even some of the scientists.

I didn't much care for the story: It was trite and the characters cliché, but I'll never forget the ocean or the ornate deck of *The Cutlass*, named for the captain's curved sword. I had never been to the ocean, but I swear I could smell the salt on the wind. When I was reading, I was there, in another world—one as real to me as home, school, Millie's house, or the magical woods behind it.

Naturally, I lost time. Late nights reading (or sometimes playing on my phone) turned into late mornings waking up. Sometimes I wasn't out the door until the sun was already high in the sky.

I didn't think Shoan minded at first. He just seemed happy to see me and happy to play.

Sometimes instead of tossing rocks into the stream or taking naps with old-man rock, I would read or play games on my phone. Shoan would lay down patiently or nap (always just out of reach) as he always did beside old-man rock.

Then one day while I was reading, Shoan wandered away. I hadn't even seen him leave.

In a panic, I pocketed my phone and searched for him. I'm not sure where he went, but he must have heard me calling for him because a minute later he was standing on the side of a tree and looking at me upside down.

So I played with him, chased him and ran from him as we always had done, and he seemed happy.

* * *

Changing Worlds

All Things Change

High school was even more complicated. I had more schoolwork. There was summer reading. There were boys. I made more friends. I got a job making pizza on the weekends.

Meanwhile, I got lost not just in my own teenage world but in the world's that others had written. I spent so much time reading that I spent so little time writing. My own made-up worlds felt so small next to those written by others.

Soon the only time I wrote was at my Aunt Millie's, and even then I wasn't writing much.

I'm sure my aunt noticed that I was writing less and less. I would dodge her questions about what I had been writing while I was at home—because I wasn't working on anything. I'm sure she noticed because eventually she stopped asking.

Bless her because she never once gave me crap about it. She never once made me feel guilty.

Looking back, I wonder if it was because she was afraid to push me away. I was a teenager, already on the dock and already in the boat—I think she was afraid I would sail away and our summer weeks together would end.

I think I was afraid of that too.

Late nights in other worlds, with friends, or in social media turned into late mornings. It didn't much matter if I was at home or in the mountains.

At my aunt's, I would still go out into the woods and run with Shoan, chase and be chased, but a little less each time. I would take pictures of the woods and the stream and old-man rock to share with friends. I tried taking a picture of Shoan a few times, but he was so fast that even when I managed to catch him he turned out like a blurry patch of green.

I would walk slow and talk with friends and with boys. I read more and played on my phone instead of napping at old-man rock or tossing pebbles into the stream.

Shoan noticed, because when I sat still he left more and more. Soon it stopped startling me when I would look around and find him missing. When I stood up and started walking he always came back to me, so I didn't think to worry.

Shoan walked with me when I went into the woods, but we no longer played. He laid down with me when I stopped by the stream and by the rock, but he didn't stay anymore.

I imagined that he went off into his own world while I went off into mine—but I no longer tried to imagine what world he ran off to.

It was that Summer of my eleventh grade year—the last day of my visit and the last week I would visit that year—that I noticed something wrong with Shoan.

That last day, I was walking through the woods and texting my boyfriend at the time. So involved in that world that I hadn't seen Shoan walking beside me.

He was still the same magical fey that he had always been, but now he seemed smaller and his bark-like skin less pronounced. His vines weren't the same twisted mass they once were. Now they were smoother, more of a cross between fur and vines.

When I saw him, I smiled and ran, but he didn't chase me. Shoan just stared and panted at me, looking at me with his eyes the color of shifting autumn. So I turned to chase him. This time he ran, but only enough to stay just out of reach. He didn't zoom and dart from tree to tree like he had before.

I only heard his rumbling laugh once all that summer.

I wanted to ask my Aunt Millie about Shoan and what might've happened to him, but I didn't. My mother came to pick me up and I spent my senior year of high school in other worlds.

Shoan and the magical forest behind my aunt's house had never been further from my mind.

That summer after I graduated, I worked full-time to save up money for college and so I only went to my Aunt Millie's house one time. Only for a long weekend.

I drove myself there, with a map app to guide me and car radio to keep me company. It was a time to think and to reminisce. I thought a lot about those woods and about my aunt.

That car ride by myself marked a turning point for me, ever so small of one. Up until then I hadn't chosen to go to the mountains; my mother had chosen to take me. Now I was choosing to go. I wanted to see mountains, the magical forest. I hoped Shoan would run with me again. I hoped it would be like old times.

That week it rained almost every day, but midway through I couldn't help myself—I ran out into the woods in the pouring rain. Within moments I was soaked, shirt and jeans clinging to me like a second skin, shoes squishing as I ran through the forest.

"Shoan!"

The rain drowned out my voice as I called out to him.

Even though it was summer, the mountain air was crisp and before long I was shivering, arms crossed feebly over my chest.

"Shoan!"

A part of me began to wonder if I had made up the green fey fox all this time. Maybe Shoan was just the wild imagination of a silly little girl.

Then I saw him. He was curled up in his green vines, hanging under a large low branch of a tree, defying gravity just as I remembered. He was nearly close enough to touch. I walked up and stood under the branch with him, hoping naively that it would keep at least a little rain off of me.

Shoan looked so small now. His skin was still the color of brown bark and water ran down the ridges of his skin. His tangled vines were no longer tangled. They were thin and the texture of grass. He seemed to be losing his magic or perhaps he was just growing old as animals did on much shorter scales than people.

He no longer panted or smiled the way he did when we would play. Shoan just stared at me with his autumn eyes, as if to say: *Silly girl, did you really think things would be the same?*

Yes, yes I did. I want to run and play like we used to.

Can't you see it's raining out. Come back again when it's dry and warm.

I'm afraid it will rain all week.

Come back another week.

But how could she explain to the tiny forest fey that she could not come back another week? How could she explain the city she lived in and the tangle obligations of work and school, and the dozen other worlds that competed for her attention.

You are a silly fox and I am a silly girl.

Shoan smiled at that.

That was the last time I saw him smile.

It did rain all week and I couldn't bring myself to go back out to Shoan.

I wish I could say that week was the week I regained my love of writing but it wasn't. I spent time on my phone and connecting with friends. I read while my Aunt Millie wrote.

The one good thing that came out of that rainy week was that I got to talk more with my Aunt Millie than I ever had in the past. We would talk in the kitchen, just like her and my mom used to do when mom dropped me off. We talked about growing up and about boys, about school and about books we loved.

I never asked about her books. I couldn't bring myself to ask about them because it reminded me that I *used* to write.

The day after I saw Shoan, Millie brought the subject up anyway. I mostly listened.

We had coffee that morning and she talked about how she made characters, with a dash of people she knew and characters from other books that she liked; the pieces coming together like coffee grounds, water, heat sugar and creamer to make a satisfying cup of coffee.

At lunch she told me about ideas, not where they came from, but how to cultivate them. She said the best books start with a question and the key to making them grow was to ask more questions. What is the world like? What if this character was the reader's eyes in the story, or what about another character?

At dinner she told me about endings and how the best endings are the ones you can see coming from a mile away. If you look close enough you will see the ending in the opening lines, in the characters, even in the title. "Especially twist endings," she said, "A twist only works if you set it up properly."

The rest of the week we talked about stories we loved and about what they meant to us. She gave me a dozen books to read and I am proud to say that she wrote down some of mine too.

All those summer weeks spent with my Aunt Millie and I felt like I was getting to know her for the first time. For the first time we were sharing worlds instead of just sitting in each other's world.

Leaving at the end of that rainy week was one of the hardest things I've done.

* * *

Lonely Worlds

I wish I could say that one week at my Aunt Millie's was the week that everything changed for me. That would make a nice, neat turning point, wouldn't it?

The next three years passed in a blur. I went away to college and got a business degree. I had internships over the summers and filled the time in between with social worlds. I didn't read much at all and I didn't write. By that point I hadn't written in years.

I wish I could say that I thought often of my Aunt Millie or of Shoan the fey fox, but I didn't think of them at all. There's no time for idle thoughts or reminiscing when you're filling all your hours of the day.

I talked to my Aunt Millie on the phone each Christmas, but it was always catching up and never again what we had that last week at her house.

My Aunt Millie passed away the year I was supposed to graduate. She was only fifty-six.

It was almost spring.

The funeral service was at a small church an hour away. We couldn't go to her house because there was still snow. An equally small group gathered to mourn, just family mostly and a few other writers she was close to over the years.

The estate was settled, book rights and royalties divided up, and Millie's house was sold all before I finished my senior year.

I never got to go back to her house. Aunt Millie had always been far away, easily a four hour drive, but now she was gone and I would never get her back. I imagined Shoan and the river and old-man rock in their own world, now impossibly far apart from mine.

I wish I could say that Aunt Millie's death was a turning point for me, or that graduating college was a turning point, but life is rarely as neat as fiction. I drifted through so many worlds and others drifted through mine. Three jobs in my twenties, two apartments, three boyfriends worth mentioning, but thankfully the same friends.

If there was a turning point for me, it was when I started reading the books that Aunt Millie wrote.

I started with *Pirates of Lochlann.* Somehow I remembered the first story to grab me was a pirate story and thought it a good place to begin—I was right. Instead of playing on my phone during free minutes, I bought the Ebook and scrolled through it. The last time I read for fun was months ago and I couldn't tell you the last book I finished.

I read the first *Pirates* book in a weekend and it only took that long because I had to work Saturday. For the first time in years, I stepped out of my own world and into another. I lost myself on the deck of the *The Crimson Storm*, in the salty spray of the Caribbean Sea, and barked orders at the crew when a frigate of the Imperial Navy bore down on them.

I found pieces of Millie inside:

The captain was fond of strawberries, and always bartered or bought fresh strawberries when they could be had; Aunt Millie's kitchen was filled with strawberries, though they were ceramic dishes with strawberries on them, strawberry jars for sugar, shakers for salt and pepper.

They picked up shipwrecked passengers and the injured were given quilts and blankets from India, with intricate mandalas woven into them; I imagined they were the same ones designs as the blankets that hung on the back of Millie's couch.

One of the shipwrecked passengers was an author, Juliette, a woman of the same wispy build as my aunt, though unaccustomed with the silence of Millie's house. Juliette was a hard woman, who didn't shy away from advocating for her "rescued crew". As the story went on, it was Juliette's mannerisms that reminded me of my aunt: Chewing her lip while she was deep in thought, bouncing her leg while she ate, even twirling her pen between sentences while she wrote.

Several times I teared up, not for anything sad but for things lost that I was reclaiming: My Aunt Millie, other worlds, and even myself, I suppose.

Immediately I started the next book.

* * *

Reclaiming Old Stories

It wasn't until two years later that the idea occurred to me.

I had already read through my Aunt Millie's entire catalogue two times and read a dozen more books. I lost myself in worlds and I had never been happier.

It wasn't until my friends suggested we go camping. We were all city boys and girls and none of us had spent a night outside in a tent; it seemed like the thing to do. We were all in our mid-twenties and working our way through our quarter life bucket lists.

I knew just the place to go.

My heart pounded as I searched for a campground near my aunt's old house. I thought of Shoan, my old friend the fey fox, for the first time in years.

John suggested another campground, but I adamantly disagreed. I think they could all hear it in my voice.

Three weeks later we were packed into my Corolla, trunk packed full with a tent and sleeping bags, and driving up to the mountains—nearly the same exact drive to Millie's old house. I actually missed the turn for the campground because I was following the old route.

We pulled into the Vinley campground. The trees were the same towering oaks that surrounded my aunt's house, but I wasn't used to seeing the people—all the people. It was midday and it seemed like everyone was back at their spots eating lunch. I gave up counting how many families were there in their RVs and pop-out trailers and tents.

Inwardly, I mocked those families that came wrapped in technology—even though I had never slept in these woods outside of a house.

At some point my stomach turned and I thought I made a mistake coming here, coming to this crowded campground on the ass-end of my Aunt's woods—a pale imitation of a sacred childhood place.

We parked, and John, Louisa and Antony waved to our new neighbors while I fumbled awkwardly with my feelings.

Louisa suggested we walk the trails and see the forest. Thankfully the others agreed.

I felt better the farther we got away from the campsite. As the voices receded, I found myself drifting back to old memories of exploring some other side of the same forest. I tried to look off into the forest or up as much as possible so that I didn't notice the paved trail we walked on.

On this side of the forest, the mountains were obnoxiously apparent. Many trails had cliffside views of the mountains. While my friends stopped and took pictures, I found myself looking the opposite direction—off into the depths of the forest.

It was an absurd thought, but I kept looking for Shoan. I kept hoping to see his green, viney fur clinging to one of the towering trees. I kept hoping to hear his rumbling laugh, like rolling thunder.

I never saw Shoan again, not that weekend in the woods or any other, but that didn't stop me from looking for him.

Three hours later we finished one of the trails and went back to our campsite. After several tries, we set up our tent and filled it with our sleeping bags. John went off to purchase fire-wood and then we sat around the first fire any of us had made. We drank and talked, much the same as we would have in an apartment, only huddling around a fire and sitting on benches.

I made a toast to my Aunt Millie and the woods I grew up in, more because I felt that I should than because I had any-thing profound to say. I thanked her for those wonderful summers and apologized for not appreciating them more as I got older.

In my head, I apologized to Shoan for not appreciating his world more while I was in it.

It wasn't until we and most of the other campers around us had turned in that things changed for me.

I couldn't sleep and so I laid awake in our tent, debating whether to hide under my sleeping bag and read. How many others around me were lying awake like I was, kicking them-selves for not bringing a softer mat to sleep on? How many were lying awake and kicking themselves for getting dragged into camping?

How many campers had been in these woods before? Were they veteran campers that traveled the country or were they on a yearly family outing?

Were these woods a cherished place to them like they were for me? Were they out here in familiar woods that had become strange and foreign to them; were they out here trying to re-claim lost memories of camping-past—lost stories? Stories near and dear to them, desperately trying to get them back.

How many of them were kicking themselves for being away for so long?

I knew the desperation of trying to reclaim old stories.

Sometimes that desperation came quietly—in silent wishes as we're falling asleep. Sometimes it came in heaving sobs beneath the torrent of the shower. Other times it was in the car running errands and I cursed myself for wearing makeup and forgetting my sunglasses.

Remembering someone dear to us and writing down a story are similar. Our distant memories and stories in our head seem so grand, but they also fade.

My summers of running and chasing Shoan were condensed into feelings. I doubt I could remember the paths we took and feared I couldn't remember the way to the stream or to old-man rock. My Aunt Millie was destined to become the same; eventually I would only remember the strawberries of her kitchen, or sitting next to her while we wrote together. Maybe condensing our loved ones was a way to keep them real.

Remembering someone dear to us and writing down a story are similar, but reversed. A person is real when they're alive and fade after, while a story is vague in our minds and only real when we write it down.

I think that for a long time I was afraid. Afraid of putting the stories in my head down on paper. Afraid that they wouldn't live up to my imagination from all those years ago. When a story isn't real—when it's in your head—it seems limitless and intangible. The goal of writing is to make it real, to put words to it and capture it on the page. Of course the story would never be as humongous on that tiny page as it was in my head—but even if it was just a sliver, just an afternoon in the woods compared to a childhood of summers—it would still be so, so worth it just to run again.

I may not be able to get my aunt back, or Shoan, but writing was the one thing I could get back.

That night in the tent under the ass-end of those cherished woods, I hid under my sleeping bag and pulled out my phone. I started to type out a story. For the first time in years I started to run again.

I lost someone magical… I think it was a part of myself.
But I'm trying to get it back.

END

Thank you for Reading

I hope you enjoyed reading these stories as much as I enjoyed writing them. If you did, I would greatly appreciate a short review on Amazon or your favorite book website. Reviews are crucial for any author, and even just a line or two can make a huge difference.

On writing *Reclaiming Near and Dear Stories*

I suppose the title is pretty on the nose, isn't it?

Growing up is inevitably about losing things: Innocence, loved ones, friends, childhood stomping grounds, plans... The narrator in *Reclaiming Near and Dear Stories* loses most of those things, but the story is mainly about that last one. Plans.

We all have dreams of what we want to be when we grew up. For me, I had brief stints with paleontology and marine biology. My first foray into college I tried psychology. But no matter what subject caught my eye or what career I thought about, writing was always there.

I wrote my first story when I was in 6th grade. Within a month or three, I had 30,000 words of a superhero story. Even though I lost that original file when my parents' computer crashed, I never stopped writing. Writing was the one constant dream in my life.

But it stayed a dream. No one goes to college for dreams. No one I knew had a dream job. People I knew pursued careers that paid a decent wage. Retirement plans, opportunities for advancement, and if you were lucky, a rewarding day-to-day grind.

I tried publishing an iteration of that superhero story in my early 20's. I sold a few copies to family and friends. It was disheartening and, if I'm being honest, the story wasn't ready to be published. I kept writing, but I shelved my dreams of publishing for most of that decade of my life. I focused on a career, got certifications and a promotion. I went back to school. That time for computer programming. Didn't finish that time either.

Eventually I met my wife and her three kids, and got married. Went back to school and finished (English, no less).

All the while I kept writing. Writing stayed a dream. And sometimes dreams get relegated to the nightstand beside the bed. Tucked away. Never forgotten… just *away*.

I told my wife about all this one day around 2018. She had seen me writing. It was right about the time I started seriously considering publishing again. I told her the story about 6th grade me writing that superhero story. She informed me that wasn't something that normal 6th grade kids did. Normal 6th graders don't sit down for month-long stretches and write stories in their spare time.

I think I said, "Huh," in realization. Something understated like that. In the months and years to follow, I've written at least a million words. To adopt a meme, it ain't much (to some prolific authors), but it's honest work.

I know that the only thing harder that putting a dream away in the nightstand is taking it back out—realizing that you owed it to yourself all along to grab your dream and run as far and as fast as you can with it.

Connect with the Author

If you want to stay up to date on the latest about Samuel's publishing news and blog, check out his website and consider signing up for his monthly newsletter.

www.SamuelFlemingBooks.com

Samuel can also be found on Goodreads and Facebook.

Samuel Fleming is a Science Fiction and Fantasy author.

He grew up in Maryland, spending most of his time swimming and writing. Swimming gave him a lot of time to daydream, so the two hobbies complemented each other well. Idle dray dreams turned into stories, some of which stuck with him for years. These days he swims a little less and writes a lot more.

He loves a good story no matter the medium: Books, TV, video games, comics, tabletop RPG's, or podcasts–most of which he attempts to share with his wife and three kids, and occasionally on his blog.

www.ingramcontent.com/pod-product-compliance
Lightning Source LLC
Chambersburg PA
CBHW030756110726
47900CB00008B/2631